# LARRY

by Lillian Budd

illustrated by Leonard Vosburgh

DAVID McKAY COMPANY, Inc.    NEW YORK

Also *by* LILLIAN BUDD

*One Heart, One Way*

*April Snow*

*Land of Strangers*

*April Harvest*

*The Pie Wagon*

*The Bell of Kamela*

*Tekla's Easter*

*The People of Long Ago Street*

*Calico Row*

*Library of Congress Catalog Card No. 66-16047*

To Guy, who writes to me

## PART ONE

Larry Bingham was the youngest.

Beside Larry, and Pop and Mom, there were four boys and four girls.

And beside all the Binghams there was Larry's dog, Teddy-R.

Whenever Larry shouted for him to come he would call him Ted, for short, but his name was really Teddy-R.

They all lived in a little cabin in the Winding Valley between the steep hills. On one steep side was the Tall Tree Woods, and on the other side was the Deep Dark Woods.

They called it the Hill Country, but it was mountain country, sure enough.

Every winter's night when supper was
done and dishes were washed and stacked
away on shelves in the pine cupboard with
the pierced tin fronts, punched out in heart
design, they would all gather around in the
Big Hall.

They called it the Big Hall, but it was
nothing more than the only room in the
cabin. That is, the only room beside the loft,
up under the eaves.

From fall to spring, every evening it was
the same. As if Mom were a magician on a
stage, ready to bring on the main act of a
show, she would go to the corner back of the
big black stove and reach for the knot on
the end of a rope that hung from the ceiling.
She would give a little yank on the rope, and
to the tune of squeaking little wheels, down
would come the ceiling!

Not really the ceiling, but almost as big as the whole ceiling. It was the quilting frame.

And then Mom and the girls would take chairs, or wooden apple crates, and sit around the frame. Mostly the quilt pattern was the "Green Pine Tree." Even to Cissy, the littlest girl, who was only a year older than Larry, they'd up the needles, down the needles, run the needles, pull the thread. And sing.

With boys on each side of him Pop would sit in one corner on the wide-board floor with his long legs bent up like a jackknife. And his blue jeans would crawl way up to show his hairy legs atop the long black woolen socks that Cissy had learned to knit on.

Pop would take up his homemade dulcimer, and he would play.

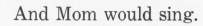
And Mom would sing.

And he would sing.

And the girls would sing.

And the boys would sing.

And Teddy-R would sing.

Then Pop would play Larry's favorite:

"Teddy-R was a good young dog,
    We thought he'd treed a squirrel.
But when we come to find it out
    He was only barkin' at the world."

Teddy-R would make as if he took a bow. Then he would lie down and make himself into a pillow for Larry. And the first thing you know Larry didn't hear the mountain tunes, like "Over the River, Charlie," and "Killy Kranky," and "Farewell, Dear Rose Annee."

Dreaming came easy for Larry when he had his head on the pillow that was Teddy-R and all around was singing-music and family love — keeping him warm.

When the quilting time was over and the
songs sung out, Pop would carry Larry up
into the loft where the girls slept. And there
he would wake up the next morning when
the sun, or rain, or snow came dribbling
through the light cracks between the shake-
shingles.

After he once turned seven he would be
allowed to sleep in the hayloft, out in the
barn, that was the bedroom for the big boys.
Like his brother, Harry.

Harry Bingham was the oldest.

You had to be almost a man — with your seventh birthday behind you, instead of not coming for almost a year yet — to sleep out where Harry slept, and the other boys.

His big brother, Harry, knew everything.

Harry was the one who had taught him how to swim, how to shoot, how to tell poison ivy from woodbine, and how to know when the trillium would bloom, and when to stand stock still to let a doe come apple-picking off the orchard floor. And how, when the clouds were "mackerel" up there in the sky it sure-as-Fate was going to rain. And what kind of bait to use to catch the biggest fish.

Maybe Mom had helped a little, but it was really Harry who had taught him to sing, too. Every night Harry would sit alongside of him and squeeze him around the shoulders a bit whenever he sang right well.

Every night had been the same: as long as Larry could remember, it was quilting and singing and singing and quilting, and love, the whole live-long time that the hush of winter's snow and cold was on the world.

But tonight was different. Maybe because spring was coming.

Maybe....

Harry was not sitting next to him, tonight, squeezing his shoulder a bit.

Mary-Lou, from back of the mountain, had come over and Harry was sitting next to her. Squeezing her around the waist, he was, whether she sang or not. Or whether, when she sang, her singing was good or not.

She had come bringing with her another pattern for the quilting time, "The Double Wedding Ring."

"Why doesn't Mary-Lou go home? Why did she have to come here anyway?" he asked, but no one paid any attention. So Larry sat alone, and he was sad.

Pop was playing, but Larry didn't like the songs. The only songs tonight were foolish songs, with no sense to them at all, not "Teddy-R was a good young dog," or about the McCoys, or any of those.

Harry was singing a solo now.

"I love Mary-Lou fondly,
 I love Mary-Lou true,
I love Mary-Lou with all my heart,
 And Mary-Lou loves me too."

Then Mary-Lou answered with,

"I am Harry's darling,
 I am Harry's pride,
And the day is not far distant
 When I'll be Harry's bride."

Larry listened. His mind could hear the words all right. The songs came out about darling and pride and love and handsome, all right, but by the time they reached his ears they had turned into the sorrow-songs, like "Wearin' the Willow" and "Grief For My Own."

That's all he could hear, for thinking about Harry's going to leave the cabin and going off with Mary-Lou to build a cabin of their own.

Larry tried to swallow, but the lump there in his throat wouldn't let him.

What was *he* going to do, with Harry gone? He would no longer have his big brother to sit alongside of as they spent the winter evenings with the quilting and the singing.

Harry wouldn't be here to teach him anything, either.

Harry had taught him everything he knew so far. Well, almost everything. But now his big brother was going away with Mary-Lou. And *he* would never learn another thing — most likely — as long as he lived.

And it was all on account of Mary-Lou. He wished she had stayed back of the mountain.

Teddy-R made himself into a pillow. But Larry didn't put his head on it. Instead, here in this room where love was shining and quilting and singing made a happy time, Larry walked straight over to Mary-Lou. He put his face close up to her pretty face and said, "I don't like you!"

In the awful quiet that came then, he went to climb the narrow worn-down stairs to the loft where he and the girls slept.

He looked around, just once. But they weren't even looking his way. Not a one of them was looking his way.

# PART TWO

It was the middle of the night.

The pitter-pat of cold spring rain was on the whole outdoors. Mom and Pop were sleeping sound. The girls in the loft were sleeping sound.

Larry's bare feet pit-a-patted down the worn-down stairs.

Teddy-R pit-a-patted at his heels past Mom and Pop, both sleeping sound.

Out of the door, into the night, into the Winding Valley between the Tall Tree Woods and the Deep Dark Woods went Larry. He was going away. Far, far away.

Just think of it: Harry had not even looked his way when he went up to bed. Nor had Mom, nor Pop, nor any of them — boys nor girls.

They would never miss him. Especially Harry would never miss him — Harry going to leave, to marry Mary-Lou.

With his heart dragging from the heel-ends of his feet Larry started toward the darkness of the Tall Tree Woods. Teddy-R trotted after him.

Larry stopped.

Teddy-R stopped.

*Anybody* could go wandering in the Tall Tree Woods. That was nothing.

Larry turned away from the Tall Tree Woods. He shivered like a young and lacy aspen tree: it was into the deeper darkness of the Deep Dark Woods a sorrowing boy should go. . . .

There was that lump in his throat again, keeping him from swallowing. And was it his heart that was hammering like a blacksmith's hammer at his chest bone?

He took a few steps.

Teddy-R took a few steps.

No. He couldn't go into the Deep Dark Woods. Why, he wasn't turned seven, yet, so he could sleep in the hayloft where big boys slept. He wasn't big enough to go into the Deep Dark Woods alone.

He stopped.

Teddy-R stopped.

But . . . Harry was going to leave the cabin . . . going to leave him. . . .

Larry made himself as tall as he could stretch. He walked past the first few trees of the Deep Dark Woods.

"HOOT — TOOT!" a night owl screeched.

He wasn't afraid of hoot-owls. With his head held high, and his heart pounding hard against his chest bone, he walked straight into the deepness of the Deep Dark Woods.

Teddy-R followed at his heels. The noises of night were their only company: the hoot-owl's hoot, the cracking of a twig, the padded foot-fall of a small wild four-footer, the echo of his own footsteps, to make him think he heard something tracking him — a bear, maybe — only a little way behind. . . .

Staring straight ahead into the night, he stooped and patted his dog. The scarey sound had to be only an echo; Teddy-R would bark if there was really something there he didn't know.

Larry shivered. He wouldn't dare to turn and look, to make sure, because he was AFRAID.

The cold spring rain ran down his cheeks. Hot rain of tears joined the cold spring rain and drops of both ran down his cheeks. He started running — stumbling blindly — away from the sound.

Then he fell.

Teddy-R stopped. He tried to speak, but only a whimper came. Then round and round he went, as his wild forefathers had done to make a sleeping place amid tall grasses. He made himself into a pillow, and Larry laid his head on it.

Dreaming didn't come to Larry now, lost as he was in the deepness and darkness of the Deep Dark Woods with the sound coming closer — closer —

If only he was at home . . . if only one of his family was near him . . . any one of them . . . it didn't have to be Harry!

He stopped crying. He almost stopped breathing, for the footstep sound came right alongside of him and stopped.

Arms went around him.

He knew they were Cissy's arms as soon as she said, "I heard when you came down on the creaky second step, so I followed you."

Her face was shining, even in the dark, the way the rounded tops of the mushrooms were glistening, from the wetness of the cold spring rain.

"I'm not mad, Cissy. I'm not mad you followed me." He wasn't mad, the way he had been on that first day he'd gone to school, when she had followed him and made him feel like a baby. He had never been so glad to see anybody in his whole life as he was to see Cissy now.

"I know why you are running away," Cissy said. She waited a moment and then asked:

"Remember the robin's nest, Larry?"

"Uh-huh." He brushed the rain and tears from his cheeks on to the sleeve of Cissy's nightgown.

"The young ones left the nest, remember? We watched them learn to fly away."

"Uh-huh."

Only the sound of breathing, and night noises, there in the pine-smelling forest, till Cissy said, "Teddy-R left his parents and sisters and brothers."

It was as if a great light, as bright as sun, came to help Larry see what he had not been able to figure out before. With his face buried in wet fur, he talked to Teddy-R. "If you hadn't left your family home I would never have had my dog!"

Teddy-R found the way home for them
and, as usual, Cissy and Larry were in their
beds in the loft when the family woke up
the next morning.

He didn't tell that he had gone out wandering in the night, nor that Cissy had come and helped him to know that it was right for the young ones, when they grew up, to leave their parents' homes. But the others didn't know he knew, so weren't they surprised when that evening he went up to Mary-Lou, and, without being told to do so, he apologized and asked her to forgive him for saying what he had said.

There was a lightning flash of understanding in the looks that passed between Mom and Cissy, and Pop and Cissy.

Then Mom came over and hugged him. And Harry and Pop looked his way, proud.

And so, that night, when the bloom of spring and love was on the whole outdoors, and indoors too, Larry and Pop and Mom and all the other Binghams, and Mary-Lou, and Larry's dog, Teddy-R, gathered around in the Big Hall.

Mom stood as if she were a magician on a stage and reached for the rope that would let the ceiling down.

Not really the ceiling, but the quilting frame.

And as the needles up'd and down'd, and ran, and the thread was pulled, there was the singing. And Pop, sitting in one corner on the wide-board floor playing his dulcimer, with his pants' legs crawled clear up to show his knees almost.

Then came Larry's favorite piece: and,
after, Teddy-R made as if he took a bow.
And then he spread out on the floor and
made himself into a pillow.

Dreaming came easy for Larry when he had his head on the pillow that was his dog, and all around was singing-music and family love, keeping him warm.

But he never dreamed of the thing that happened to him this night. He didn't even know it till the morning.

When morning came, he woke to see the sun dribbling through the light cracks between the shingles, and he saw that he had been carried, while asleep, not to the loft room up under the eaves of the cabin where the girls slept. Pop had carried him out to the hayloft, in the barn, where only big boys slept.